THE PRIVATE CLUB

BOOK TWO

J.S. COOPER & HELEN COOPER

CHAPTER ONE

"Just be quiet." The man removed his hand from my mouth. "I'm not going to hurt you."

I listened to his voice and shivered, pushing him away roughly as I rubbed my lips aggressively, trying to remove the taste of him from my mouth.

"I don't care what you have going on, Brandon. I am not going to let this complicate everything. Get your ass down here." Greyson's voice was harsh as we listened to him through the door. "We have things we need to take of."

I stood there in the dark, biting my lip hard. I was scared to be in this room with a stranger, but I was even more scared of what might happen if Greyson knew I had heard his call. Was I the new girl he had been talking about? Was that why Greyson was playing with me? Did he have darker intentions where I was concerned? My body shivered again and the man next to me grabbed me.

"Let go!" I hissed and pushed him again. "Who are you?"

"All your dreams come true." He laughed loudly, and I wondered if I was with a crazy man.

"Turn the lights back on."

"Want to be able to see my face when you kiss me?"

"I don't want to kiss you."

"Oh, only Greyson gets that honor?"

I gasped at his words and stood there in shock as the lights went back on. David, the head security guard, was standing in front of me. I stared at him in confusion. I had been positive that I'd been taken advantage of by Frank.

"You." My eyes narrowed as I stared at his stocky build. How could I have thought, even for one second that he was Greyson? "Why did you find me in here and kiss me?" I tried not to look too disgusted. I didn't want him to get angry.

"I shouldn't have kissed you. I'm sorry." His eyes looked apologetic, but I didn't feel like forgiving him. "I couldn't resist." He shrugged. "You're beautiful."

"That doesn't answer my question. Why did you follow me in here?"

"You're in danger. I had to warn you," he whispered and came closer to me.

"How would you know?" I frowned at him, but my heart was racing. What if he was telling the truth?

"Meg, I'm an undercover cop." He gave me a wry smile. "I've been working here undercover for the last two years."

"Undercover?" I looked at him carefully to see if he was telling the truth. I'd taken some body language classes at a community college when I was in law school and I knew most of the telltale signs of a liar: shifty eyes unable to make eye contact, constant licking of the lips or lip biting, playing with hands or hair, foot tapping, wide smile, and wide eyes. But David exhibited none of those signs. He looked me directly in my eyes and his shoulders were straight.

"I work for the vice squad in the New York Police Department." His eyes were serious now and his voice was low. "I'm trusting you're not going to let anyone in on what we're doing here?"

"I don't know what you're doing." I shook my head and stepped back.

"Don't play stupid, Meg. We both know you're a smart girl."

"How do you know my name?" I was staring at him, but my ears were still perked up to hear what was happening outside of the door.

"I know all of the girls' names."

"You know what I mean." I stepped towards him now. "Why did you come in here? Why share this information with me? You don't even know me."

"I know that you used to be a lawyer. I could use your help."

"What help?"

"Everything is getting out of control here. We need someone on the inside to help us."

"You are on the inside. You're the frigging head of security."

"I don't know what's going on." He looked at me with a worried expression. "Twining is careful. Very careful. He doesn't let us see what happens after the tests."

"What do you mean?"

"The girls disappear." His voice was low. "They all just disappear."

"What?" My voice was loud and his hand flew to my mouth.

"Shh," he whispered angrily. "We don't want to alert anyone to the fact that I'm in here."

"Greyson may come in," I told him reluctantly. "He's come into my last two test rooms. He may come in here as well."

"He's really taken a liking to you, hasn't he?" He looked me over in surprise.

"Why is that so surprising to you? Am I not his usual type?"

"I don't know his usual type. He doesn't normally come around the girls." He scratched his head. "That's another reason why I need your help. There's something about you that intrigues him. You need to get us answers."

"What answers am I supposed to get?"

"We think that Greyson is involved in some sort of prostitution ring. He's grooming these young girls for rich men all over the world."

I shook my head. "I don't believe it."

"Don't you wonder what happened to Maria?"

"Maria?" My heart stopped as he said her name. How did he know about Maria? And more importantly, which Maria was he talking about?

"Your roommate Nancy's sister?"

"How do you know that Nancy had a sister?"

"I told you. I know everything." His voice was slightly angry this time.

"I don't really understand what you expect me to do."

"Just keep getting close to Greyson. Try and find out what your job is going to be."

"Won't he just send me off with the other girls, though?"

"You're too old." David looked apologetic as his words crushed down on me. "These men, they want young girls, girls they can mold. You've got your own mind. Now that you're older, you would never be a desired woman."

"Well, thanks."

"These men are sick, Meg. They want weak, pliant women. That's how they get off."

"So this is some sort of sex trade thing going on?" I frowned. "It doesn't make sense to me."

"I don't know all the answers." He sounded angry that I wasn't taking him one hundred percent at his word. "That's why I came to you."

"Why did you kiss me?"

"Because I like you and you're hot." He grinned. "I'm still a man, after all."

I thought back to the conversation I'd overheard earlier. "So are Frank and Elizabeth working with you as well?"

"What? No?" He frowned. "Why would you think that?"

"No reason." I walked over to the desk and started picking up files. My brain was racing a million miles a minute. There was no way that David was working with Frank and Elizabeth, which meant that they were up to something else—

maybe something even more sinister, if that were possible. "What about Brandon Hastings?" I looked back at him. "What role does he have in this?"

"We think he's on the outside, getting the johns lined up for the girls." David looked at me in anger. "We think he's the one who corrupts the girls."

"Oh no."

"He's this rich piece of shit who preys on younger girls." David's voice was emotional, and I could see that his hands were clenched. "I can't wait until he goes away for a long time."

"Goes away?"

"To jail." His words were harsh, but when his eyes looked at me, his expression was oddly empty. "I'm not going to stop until he and Greyson are imprisoned."

"Oh." A feeling of fear surrounded me then, and I looked down at the files in my hand with heavy eyes. All of the information he'd given me was giving me a headache and a burdened heart. "Well, I'll do what I can to help." I nodded at him. "You should leave now, just in case Greyson comes in the room." I turned away from him quickly, my mouth feeling dry as I said Greyson's name. How could he be that person? Was he pure evil? He had to be, if what David said was true. He was basically trafficking women. I felt sick to my stomach. I had made out with a human trafficker. I'd let him touch me and grope me, and I'd been about to let him fuck me. My body still ached for his touch. How could I still feel this way about him, knowing what I now knew?

"I'll come to your room tonight so we can talk." David interrupted my thoughts and I wished he would just leave.

"I don't know." I shook my head. "I have a roommate." *And I don't want you to think you can touch me*, I thought to myself.

"Nancy's your roommate, right?" he asked casually and I nodded. "She's fine. We can even enlist her for help."

"Really? You trust her as well?"

"Yeah. She seems like she is trustworthy." He walked to the door. "But I better go. Remember to keep your eyes alert and your ears peeled. We'll talk tonight."

"Okay." I watched him leave the room and I felt my body relax.

I stared at the door for a few moments, trying to take in what had just happened. I couldn't believe that David was an undercover cop. Or, really, part of me didn't want to believe. Not because I cared about him or even knew him. I didn't want him to be an undercover cop because then what he had told me wouldn't seem so real. I didn't want to think that this private club was really a disguise to sell women into prostitution. I didn't know Greyson very well, but my heart didn't want to believe he could be capable of such a thing.

"Don't be an idiot, Meg," I muttered to myself. "You don't even know him."

I continued filing the folders and waited for Greyson to come and join me in the room. But he never showed. To say I was disappointed was an understatement. I wanted to see him, to look into his eyes and see if he was a monster.

The session seemed to take forever and it was extremely boring. I didn't even bother looking in folders for more clues. What was the point? I already knew what was going on here. I most probably already knew what had happened to Nancy's sister. She was most probably in some Arabic country servicing some sheikh, or maybe she was in Asia somewhere as a concubine. For all I knew, she was on a ranch somewhere in Texas, servicing some rancher on a cattle farm. Or maybe she was in a basement somewhere in Manhattan, locked away from sight, being visited every night by her 'master' while his wife slept. Who knew where she was?

I'd taken some human trafficking classes in law school. I knew enough to know that you never really knew who was involved in the trade.

I took a deep breath as I felt a tear roll down my cheek. I wanted to cry. I wanted to break down on the floor and cry until I couldn't cry anymore. It was all too much. I hadn't counted on this. I could have dealt with a strip club; in fact, I'd been expecting a strip club. But this news, this new reality, was too much for me. I didn't want to be here trying to solve this problem. This was too heavy for me.

"Task completed," a voice spoke into the room to alert me that I was done with task three. I walked slowly to the door, not even bothering to wipe my eyes. I was done here. I couldn't deal with this. At the end of the day, I was still me and I couldn't deal with this. I was going to leave and then call Katie and tell her everything.

I opened the door and stepped into the corridor quickly, but I jumped when I saw Greyson standing outside the door.

"Hey." He smiled at me, his mouth curling up slightly as he looked at me.

"Hi," I spoke back to him curtly, unable to make myself smile. My heart skipped a beat as we made eye contact, but I refused to allow myself to be happy at his presence.

"What's wrong?" He walked over to me with a concerned look on his face.

"Nothing?" I shook my head and looked away from him.

"It's not nothing." His finger reached up and rubbed my wet cheeks. "You've been crying."

"No." I looked down.

"Yes." His voice was angry. "Don't lie to me. Why were you crying?"

"I wasn't crying," I lied and looked up at him. He was staring at me, and my breath caught as I saw the concern in his eyes.

"Meg, what's wrong?" His tone was softer now. "It wasn't the test, was it? You only had filing to do. That shouldn't make you cry."

"How do you know I had filing?" I looked at him suspiciously.

"Because I put you in that room and I made sure your next task was filing." He smiled at me gently before he grabbed a handkerchief from his pocket and wiped my eyes.

"Oh."

"I thought I'd surprise you after the test."

"You didn't come in."

"I told you that I wouldn't be able to stop myself if I came into the next room with you."

"But you waited outside for me?" I spoke as if I were in a daze, which I was.

"I wanted to see your face." His fingers lightly traced my lips. "I wanted to get a kiss before you went to your next test."

"Why?" I questioned him and stared into his deep blue eyes. "Why did you want to see my face?"

"Do I have to have a reason?" He raised an eyebrow. "Can't I just want to see it?"

"Yeah, you should have a reason. Most people would have a reason." My voice was sharp, and he stepped away from me.

"Are you mad at me because I didn't come into the room?" There was a hint of a smile on his lips.

I glared at him. "Really? You really think that's why I was crying?"

"I don't know. You girls are strange creatures."

"I know you think you're God's gift to women, but you're not God's gift to me."

"Pity." He laughed. "I'd quite like to give my gift to you."

"What gift?" I asked him, confused again.

"This one." He grabbed my hand and placed it on the front of his pants. "I've been told by many that it's the best gift they've ever received."

"Is that supposed to be funny or cute?" I yanked my hand away from him and tried not to think of the hard package I'd just been holding. "Because it's neither."

He frowned and looked at me seriously. "What's got you this way?"

"I'm just fed up." I shrugged. "I'm here doing stupid tests for a job I know nothing about, and it seems like I'm no closer to knowing."

"Do you really want to know?" He walked toward me again, and this time he didn't stop.

I took a few steps back to get away from him but found myself up against the wall. He walked until he couldn't walk anymore. His body was pressed against mine and the warmth of his chest heated me up.

"Yes." I nodded, wide-eyed. This was it, then. He was finally going to tell me what went on here.

"You're training to be my personal stripper." He smiled as he leaned in to kiss me. "That's why I'm taking a very personal interest in your training." He kissed me lightly on the lips.

I groaned as his tongue entered my mouth and I kissed him back eagerly. *Stop it, Meg!* I screamed at myself. *Stop it!* But I couldn't. I couldn't stop my hands from reaching up and grabbing his golden tresses. I couldn't stop myself from sucking on his tongue and adjusting my position against the door so that I could feel his hardness pressed against my lower stomach.

"I want to make love to you," he whispered against my lips.

"I thought you wanted to fuck me," I said in a blasé tone.

"I want to fuck you and then make love to you." He grinned and kissed my cheeks. "I'm glad you're not crying anymore."

"You don't really care."

"So you know me, then?" He chuckled, but his eyes looked sad as he gazed at me. "I do have a heart, you know, despite everything I've said."

"Really? I thought it was frozen. Or maybe been taken out."

"I wouldn't be surprised if my heart had been taken out at some point." He gave me a wry smile. "Maybe when I started high school."

"Maybe at the same time you realized that you'd never be a comedian?"

"Yeah, maybe." His eyes lit up and he stared at me for a few seconds. "You really listen, don't you?"

"Why wouldn't I?" I frowned.

"I don't know." He shrugged. "Most women only seem to want to talk about their own issues. I find that they don't really listen that well."

"Really?" I was surprised at his comments. "I would have thought every woman would listen to what you had to say."

"Really? Why's that?"

"Because you're hot." I laughed. "And you're mysterious. Women like a mysterious, hot man."

"Is that why you like me?"

"I like you because you're rich." I winked at him, but he didn't laugh. "I'm joking, by the way. That's not why I like you."

"So you do like me?" He sighed and took a step back. "You shouldn't like me."

"Why?"

"I'll only hurt you."

"Are you trying to hurt me?" I looked at him carefully.

"Of course not."

"Then you won't hurt me." I shrugged. "I'm not a fragile doll. I won't break."

"Is that an invitation to fuck you?" He smirked.

"Is everything about fucking to you?"

"Isn't it for you?" He stepped closer to me again and grabbed my hands. "Your fingers are trembling slightly at my touch. I know you're thinking, *What is he going to do next?* And that excites you. And maybe it slightly scares you. But it excites you more than it scares you. And you know why it excites you? It excites you because you want me to do all the things you've been thinking about in your mind but you don't want to admit. You want me to take you back into that room and you want me to fuck you. Long and hard. And I want to. I want to feel more than your fingers trembling beneath mine. But I'm not going to."

"Why not?" I whispered, eyes wide and unblinking. There was a throbbing between my legs that told me that everything he had just said was correct.

"Because now's not the time." His eyes were dark. "And you haven't begged me yet."

"I'm never going to beg you," I gasped.

"Then we will never make love." He laughed and his lips brushed mine slowly. "But for some reason, I don't think that's going to be an issue."

"I'm not going to beg you to make love to me." I shook my head energetically. "You're wasting your time if you think I'm going to beg."

"Do you think I'm sexy?"

I nodded in response.

"Do you think I can give you the best orgasm of your life?"

I nodded again slowly, unable to come up with some witty lie.

"Do you think you'll be able to resist me when I take you to the brink of that orgasm?"

I stared at him breathlessly, unsure of what he was saying.

"Do you?" His voice was urgent. "Do you think you'll be able to go to the brink of the hottest orgasm of your life and step away?"

"I don't know."

"You don't know?" His eyes narrowed and he smiled slowly. "You don't know." He laughed throatily, the sound coming from the depths of his throat. It was hearty and seductive, and I stared at him in wonder. "Oh, Meg. You're lucky you're with a man and not a boy. You may not know, but I do. I will have you screaming for me to take you."

"No, you won't," I whispered.

"Are you arguing with me?" He cocked his head.

"No." I shook my head. "But I won't be begging or screaming."

"Is that a challenge?"

"No."

"It's a challenge." His eyes lit up. "I will have you begging me and screaming for me to fuck you. And then I will wait. I will wait until you can't stand it anymore and then I will give you the best fucking of your life."

"Yeah, right." I swallowed and stepped back so that my back was against the door again. "I wouldn't hold your breath."

"I can tell you've never been with a real man before, Meg. Or you wouldn't doubt my ability to take you to the brink of heaven and make it hell."

"So you're telling me you're the devil?"

"I already told you. You shouldn't play with fire."

"Are you a good guy or a bad guy?" I sighed, suddenly overwhelmed with lust and worry.

"I'm neither. I'm just me."

"The wannabe comedian."

"The wannabe comedian." He smiled and bowed his head. "You sum me up so eloquently."

"What's my job here?" I spoke up. "And what are the other girls' jobs? What's going to happen to me? And to Nancy and to Elizabeth and the other girls?"

"I can't talk about it." His body froze and a mask fell over his face. "You won't have the same job as the other girls."

"Why not?" I frowned.

"You're special."

"Says who?"

"Says me!"

"What if I wasn't special?" I stepped towards him again, fire in my eyes. "What if I wasn't special? Would I be sent away as well?"

"Who told you that?" His voice was angry and he looked at me with sharp eyes.

"Who told me what?" I trembled with fear. Had David been correct?

"Who told you that we send the girls away?" The smile was gone from his face and all facades of flirtation were gone.

"No one." I swallowed hard. "But are they?"

"I've got to go." He gave me another look.

"Why don't you answer me, Greyson?" I reached out and grabbed his arm. "Tell me what's really going on here."

"I can't do that." He pulled his arm back and stepped away. "This isn't any of your business." He gave me a sad look. "I'm sorry, but you don't want to know too much. I've done things, Meg. I'm not a good guy." He sighed and shook his head. "Look, I have to go. If you don't think you can handle this …" He waved his hands between us. "Whatever we have, it's about sex—nothing else. You won't get anything out of me. We won't fall in love. You won't get my secrets and confidences. This is about sex. If you can't handle that, I …"

"You what?" My heart thudded with pain. His words sounded harsh and cruel. It wasn't that I thought this was about more than sex. But the way he was speaking to me, combined with the look in his eyes, made me feel sick to my stomach.

"I don't know what to say." He looked away from me. "I have to go, Meg. I'm sorry."

"No, you're not."

"You're right. I'm not." And he turned around and walked away from me.

I watched his back as he walked. I couldn't stop myself from being that pitiful girl. That girl who goes after the bad boy and then wonders why she ended up alone and confused. I was that girl. I realized that I was acting like that girl.

What did I care if all he wanted from me was sex? Who was he? For all I knew, he was a despicable human being. All signs were pointing to that.

I turned around and took a few deep breaths. I wasn't going to let him psych me out. And I wasn't going to let him sidetrack me. His whole demeanor had changed when I'd talked about the girls being sent away. His eyes had looked angry, surprised, upset, and worried. He'd looked worried. He was worried I'd report him to the authorities. He was worried I'd figure out the truth. He was trying to use my attraction to him to divert me. He'd made a mistake.

I was now more determined than ever to get to the truth.

CHAPTER TWO

"How was your day?" I asked Nancy casually as she walked into the room a good thirty minutes after all the tests had been completed.

"Long." She sighed. "Very long."

"Figure anything out yet?"

"Not really." She shook her head. "This place is like a maze."

"You went exploring?"

"Kind of." She made a face, distorting her pretty features into a grimace. "I got lost."

"I wondered where you were."

"I don't think I can do this." Her eyes looked sad. "I thought I could, but it just seems too hard. I'm no Benson."

"Who?"

"Olivia," she said, as if that made more sense.

"Sorry, I don't know who Benson or Olivia are," I said almost apologetically.

"Olivia Benson is one person."

"Oh, is she famous or something?"

"Detective Olivia Benson? She used to be partners with Stabler!"

"Nancy, I hate to break this to you, but I have no idea who Stable is either."

"Not Stable," she smiled. "Stabler. Detective Stabler. He was played by Christopher Meloni. Oh my God, he's so hot."

"Stable?"

"No, Christopher Meloni," she giggled. "Have you never watched *Law and Order: SVU*?"

"I have, actually. " I laughed.

"Well, Olivia Benson is a kickass, fearless detective. I wish I were like her, but I'm not."

"I don't think many of us are as fearless as TV characters always seem to be."

"You are." She stared at me in admiration. "You're strong and fearless."

"I don't know about that." I shrugged, but I was really feeling quite happy at her assessment of me. Maybe I was stronger than I thought. Maybe I was a warrior princess just waiting to break out.

"Did you hear about Brandon Hastings?" she gushed in excitement, her eyes alive and glowing.

"No, what about him?" I asked softly, noticing the change in her demeanor. She was upbeat now, and she was breathing fast.

"He's coming to the club."

"He is? How do you know that?"

"Huh?" She looked at me blankly and bit her lower lip. "I just heard somewhere as I was walking back to the room."

"Who did you hear?" I pretended I wasn't that interested in her answer, but I felt tense inside from waiting.

"Dunno. One of the girls." Her eyes looked past mine and she shifted uneasily. She was lying go me. I could tell she was lying to me, but I just didn't know why.

"Oh, okay." I walked back to my bed and sat down. "Do you care if he comes?"

"No, of course not," she rushed out quickly. "I don't even know him."

"So he was best friends with Greyson Twining, huh?" I asked innocently, faking ignorance. "Do you know anything else about them and the club?"

"Not much." She looked up at me and her face looked pale. She looked younger than her eighteen years as she stood there, and my heart ached for her. Whatever was going on, I had a feeling that Nancy was not the mastermind. She just didn't seem to be fully with it. And if she was, she was a mighty fine actress.

"Come and sit next to me." I got up and sat on the couch in the corner of the room and patted the space next to me. "We should talk now anyway. Try and figure out what information we have and what we should do next."

"Yeah." She sighed and walked over to me. "You really don't have to."

"I don't mind." I smiled at her.

"I don't want you to get hurt." She looked down. "This isn't a safe place."

"I can protect myself. Greyson isn't going to harm me."

"I'm just saying there are other people, you know?" She looked around the room. "I don't think that you're—"

"Hey, girls. Do you mind if I come in?" David walked into the room and gave me a tight smile.

I smiled weakly and nodded at him. *Trust him to walk in at that moment.*

"Hi, I'm David." He introduced himself to Nancy and she nodded and looked away. "What's your name?"

"Nancy." She sighed, and I could see that David's face was tense as he stared at her. I stared at him for a moment, wondering what his game was. Earlier he had known exactly who Nancy was.

"It's okay, Nancy." I stood up. "I spoke to David earlier. He may be able to help us figure out what happened to your sister."

"Your sister?" David's eyes narrowed, and I saw Nancy's face flush red.

"I'm sorry, I shouldn't have said anything. It wasn't my place." I gave David a look, but he just stared at Nancy, who still looked terrified. I was slightly confused and my heart beat rapidly. Hadn't David and I talked about Nancy's sister earlier? Hadn't he mentioned something about knowing that she had gone missing? I wanted to slap myself for forgetting exactly what we'd discussed earlier.

"What do you want?" Nancy spoke up finally, and I was surprised at the temerity in her voice.

"I came to talk to Meg. Do you mind?"

"Why would I mind?" She glared at him and his eyes narrowed.

"Just keep it to yourself," he muttered and turned to me. "So did you get anything from Greyson?"

"No, I didn't even see him again."

"Yes, you did. You saw him in the corridor."

"Are you spying on me?"

"I have eyes everywhere."

"Not really." I raised an eyebrow. "If you did, you'd know what was going on here."

"Greyson's not dumb." He shrugged. "He knows the only person he can trust is himself."

"You don't think Patsy knows?"

"I don't know." He sighed. "Her lips are tighter than a dead Catholic priest's."

"What?"

"They're not supposed to share your confessions." He spoke slowly as if I were slow.

"Okay."

"It's okay if you don't get it. You're blond, after all."

"David." Nancy's voice was shocked and she looked more affronted than I felt.

"It's okay, Nancy. He's an undercover cop with an ego. I guess you have something to prove, huh? You've been here two years and you still have no clue as to what's going on here."

"I already told you what's going on." He glared at me.

"What proof do you have?" I questioned, really wanting to know the answer to the question.

"Ask him." His voice was low. "Ask Greyson and see what he says."

"Do you really think he's going to tell me?" I rolled my eyes.

"He'll come and see you tomorrow. I'm sure of it." He stared at me. "He'll come to see you during the tests again."

"He won't come and see me tonight?" I tried not to let him see how eager I felt.

"No." He shook his head. "He would never come and visit you during the night. You're not that important to him. He'll only visit you in the day."

"I see." I felt hurt at his words but didn't disagree. I couldn't see Greyson coming to the door or window late at night either. He was no Romeo, and I was no Juliet.

"Brandon Hastings is coming tomorrow." David's eyes lit up.

"How do you know?" I stared at him and saw Nancy's face reddening as she avoided eye contact with me. I looked at Nancy and then at David and realized that there was some sort of weird tension between them. I hadn't noticed it before, but now I could definitely tell. Something wasn't right here. It wasn't a lover's tension either. It was something more than that. Something impenetrable. I shivered as I realized that they knew each other. I was sure of that. But I was also sure that they were keeping it a secret. My head started pounding again as I remembered seeing Frank and Elizabeth talking as well. What was going on here?

"I told you. I know everything." His eyes sparkled. "I know that you haven't succumbed to the Twining charm."

"What charm?" I looked at him with questioning eyes.

"You haven't fucked him yet," he said bluntly and both Nancy and I gasped at the crudeness of his words.

"I've barely been here two days."

"It doesn't take most women two minutes to rip their panties to the side for Greyson."

"I'm not most women."

"That's why I like you." He winked at me and I tried to not show him my disgust.

I didn't like David and the liberties he took with me. I was still angry about the kiss. Part of me felt like I was a hypocrite. How could I feel so uneasy around David when I craved being around Greyson? I was angry that David had kissed me without my asking, but I was craving for Greyson to do so much more. And I didn't know either of them.

"We'll talk tomorrow." I dismissed him. "You should go now."

"Don't you want to hear more about Brandon?"

"Not really." I sighed. "Not right now."

"Shit's going to go down." David smiled maliciously. "It's all going to go down now. Brandon is going to lose the love of his life."

"I thought you wanted to get Brandon and Greyson for prostitution or trafficking or whatever." My voice rose suspiciously. "Why do you care about his love life?"

"Because he doesn't deserve to be happy." David's eyes were lifeless as he looked at me. "A man like him doesn't deserve love. Neither does Greyson, but he knows it. He knows who he is. Evil bastard doesn't have a heart so he doesn't even try."

"You really hate him, don't you?"

"I hate both of them." David looked at me for a second and then his expression changed. "I can come back later tonight if you want."

"I don't want you to." I looked at Nancy. She was staring at the ground. I could tell she looked uncomfortable and she was doing everything to avoid eye contact with me.

"If you change your mind, just go to the courtyard." He licked his lips. "I'll come and find you."

"Sure." I turned away.

"Have a great evening, girls." He nodded at us and left the room.

"He's creepy," I whispered to Nancy a few seconds later and she looked at me with sad eyes.

"Everyone acts differently when presented with tragedy." She shrugged and sat on her bed. I watched as she lay back and closed her eyes. "I could sleep for a month."

"Long day, huh?"

"More like a long life." Her voice cracked and she rolled over to face the wall. I took that as a sign that she wanted to be by herself.

"I'll let you relax then. I think I'm going to go and take a shower," I spoke to her back softly. "A long, hot shower." She didn't answer, and I left the room to let her be by herself.

Even though I didn't trust that Nancy was being one hundred percent truthful to me, I did still believe that she was legitimately trying to find out what happened to her sister. Or at least that she was here because of her sister. My heart hurt for her. I wasn't sure what I would do if someone close to me disappeared. What if Katie just disappeared one day and I never knew what happened to her? I'd die. I'd move heaven and earth to find her.

As I walked down the corridor, my heart skipped a beat. What if Brandon was part of the reason why Maria had disappeared? Was he planning on doing the same thing to Katie? I'd never really liked Brandon for what he'd done to Katie. He'd broken her heart, and I'd always secretly thought he was too old for her. I mean, what thirty-five-year-old dates an eighteen-year-old? Granted, he supposedly had thought she was twenty-one, but still! Why would he have dated a twenty-one-year-old if he wasn't a creeper?

I found myself in the corridor of test rooms and quickly walked to the door that had housed the office. I'd seen a phone in there. Maybe it was actually plugged in and working. It was likely not working, but it was worth a chance. I needed to call Katie. I needed to make sure that she was okay.

CHAPTER THREE

I stepped into the shower room and was glad to see that there were no other girls in there. It had been a long time since I'd had to shower in communal showers, and I just needed to be alone with my thoughts.

Katie hadn't picked up the phone and I was slightly worried. All I could think about was what she was doing. I was worried about her.

I turned the light off so that I could shower in the dark. Something about my thoughts made me want to be surrounded by darkness. I turned on the water and adjusted it so that it was hot without being scalding. I quickly pulled off my clothes, threw them over a rail in front of all the showers, and then stepped under the water and closed my eyes, allowing the drumming to calm my mind and thoughts.

The water drops fell hard against my skin and my nerves screamed as the slightly too-hot water burned me. I didn't adjust the knob though. I wanted to be hot. I needed to think of something other than the mysteries surrounding the club, if only for a few minutes.

I wanted to think about Katie, but all I could think about was Greyson. Handsome, domineering, pompous, alluring Greyson. He'd brought out a side of me I'd never known existed. A sexual deviant had been dormant inside of me, and I wanted him to draw my inner goddess out.

I poured some body wash into my hands and rubbed it over my body, imagining they were Greyson's hands that were touching me. I rubbed my arms roughly and then my legs, making my way up to my stomach and slowing my movements. As my hands moved over my breasts, I sighed, wishing he were in there with me. I leaned back against the wall and turned my face up to the water, wishing it would sink some sense into my brain. I felt sick to my stomach. I had so much to think about, but the one thought crowding my brain was what it would feel like to make love to Greyson Twining.

A noise made my eyes pop open and I froze in the shower, listening to see if someone had walked into the shower room. I stood there with my heart beating fast. I nearly screamed when I heard definite footsteps.

"Hello?" I called out weakly. My throat felt constricted with fear, and I looked around for something I could use as a weapon.

"Meg," he said slowly and smoothly, as if he were trying to seduce me with words alone.

"Greyson?" I whispered excitedly this time. It wasn't really a question. I knew exactly who was here with me.

"Meg." He said my name again with a slow drawl. I could hear the smile in his voice and I smiled back, suddenly happy.

"What are you doing in here?" I snapped, not really angry but not wanting him to know I'd just been fantasizing about him in here with me.

"I came to see you, of course."

"How'd you know I was in here?"

"Logical deduction." I could tell from the sound of his voice that he was on the other side of the shower curtain. All he had to do was push it aside and he would see me here, naked and wet, waiting for him.

"You're Einstein, then? That was a very accurate deduction."

"Does it sound better or worse if I say I followed you here?"

"What?" My heart started pounding.

"I was coming to see you in your room, but then I saw you leaving and going to the study room. I was going to talk to you then but saw you hurrying in here. I debated with myself about coming in."

"You came to my room?" I knew I sounded shocked.

"Well, I was coming. Never made it since I saw you leave."

"Why were you coming to my room?"

"Do you really want to know?"

I shivered as I listened to him so close, yet so far. I nodded at his words but then remembered that he couldn't see me. "Yes," I said simply.

"How badly do you want to know?" His voice was soft and I swallowed. I knew what he meant.

"I want to know," I whispered back. I held my hands over my breasts as he drew the curtain back and stepped towards me.

"Hey." He smiled at me and then laughed as his saw my hands trying to cover my nakedness from him.

"Hey." I didn't smile back.

"Showering?" He took another step towards me and I stared at him with wide eyes.

"Your clothes are going to get wet," I mumbled as he walked into the shower with me—fully dressed.

"Would you rather I joined you naked?" He smirked and I shivered. His eyes narrowed as he stared at my body, and he walked closer to me until he was right in front of me and water was pouring down on him as well. "I guess I can have a clothed shower."

"You still have your shoes on." I looked down at his feet. "You can take those off."

"Thank you." He laughed while he bent down and untied his shoes. I watched as he threw them to the side and took off his socks. He looked back at me and winked. "There you go, ma'am." His face was plastered with water and the front of his hair was sticking to his forehead. I reached up and brushed it away, not thinking about my nakedness anymore. He immediately took one more step towards me and I felt his soaking-wet shirt against my nipples.

"Do you always like showering in the dark?"

"No." I shook my head and froze as I heard a sound. "You need to leave," I whispered.

"Why?" His hands rested on my shoulders.

"What if someone comes in here?" I was breathless as his hands started massaging me.

"So what?" He shrugged and bit down on my shoulder. I let out a small yelp and he laughed. "I don't care," he mumbled and kissed up my neck. My hands flew to his hair, and his chest crushed into me as he nibbled his way up to my earlobe.

"Greyson," I moaned as his tongue darted in my ear.

"Yes, Meg?" he whispered in my ear as his right hand fell to my breast.

I looked into his eyes and groaned before pressing my lips against his. This wasn't the moment for me to play games. I didn't want to be hard to get. This was my fantasy coming true and I didn't want it to stop. I kissed Greyson passionately. My body was on fire, and this time it wasn't due to the temperature of the water.

My hands left his hair and worked their way towards his shirt. My fingers pressed against his chest, and I melted as I felt his toned body beneath them. I quickly unbuttoned his shirt and my fingers flew to his wet, naked chest, running along his pecs and the silky patches of hair covering them. I pulled his shirtsleeves down and then ripped his shirt away from his wet body, letting it fall to the ground.

I went to work on his pants then, unbuckling his belt quickly and unzipping him efficiently. I pulled his pants down and he stepped out of them deftly. I stood back up and stared at his body. The only thing separating us from being completely naked together were his black briefs. I stared at the front of him and tried to ignore the fact that his cock was hard and standing at attention. My brain was able to force my eyes to look away, but my hands acted of their own accord when they reached down and held him gingerly.

I heard Greyson take a sharp breath and he pushed himself hard into my hands. I slipped my fingers into his briefs and reached down to grab him with my bare hands. He groaned then, a loud, guttural sound that turned me on even more than I was already. I grasped him eagerly, feeling brazen and confident in our mutual attraction.

Greyson might not do relationships, but I knew for a fact that he was attracted to me. Even if there was another reason behind his interactions with me, I knew he wasn't faking his desire for me. Greyson was as physically attracted to me as I was to him. I knew that that didn't really mean anything. Sex was a base, animal instinct at the end of the day, but it still made me feel proud and confident to know that a man as attractive and dynamic as Greyson was interested in me.

Greyson slammed me back into the wall and growled, "Don't go playing with fire."

"I'm not. Fire came to play with me."

"You like being a bad girl, don't you?" He sounded pleased.

"I've never been a bad girl before," I whispered as my hand went up and down his member.

"Really?" His hand slipped in between my legs easily, gliding smoothly to my pussy as his fingers sailed on the water drops and then started playing with me.

"Really!" I breathed hard as my knees buckled. His strong arms held me up, and I stared up at him with a small smile of thanks.

"For once, I think I believe you," he chuckled, and his mouth fell to my breast. His mouth suckled on my breast and I moaned. The feel of his body next to mine and the water crashing down on us had my nerve endings on high alert. Ever fiber of my body was feeling every sensation running through me.

"What does that mean?" I blinked at him. "You think I've lied to you before?"

"No," he muttered, his teeth tugging on my nipple gently. "Other women play games and pretend they're something they're not. They're lying to me and to themselves. It annoys me. But I don't think you're lying. I think you're a good girl turning bad."

"I'm not turning bad." I shook my head and then whimpered as his lips left my breast.

"You're not turning bad anymore. You *are* bad." He grinned at me and kissed me hard before pulling his briefs off.

I swallowed as I stared at Greyson, who was standing in front of me in all of his naked glory. His body was magnificent, and the drops of water only made him look sexier and more real. My fingers ran along his chest and to his abdomen. His muscles were taut, and it was only then that I realized just how strong and virile Greyson was. I'd always known he was handsome and sexy, but I'd never realized just how built he was.

His body was a muscular mass of perfection, and I groaned as I realized that I would never forget this moment. Greyson was going to ruin me for other men. A one-night or one-week dalliance with this man was going to ruin all my future relationships. I would never be able to look at another man without comparing him to Greyson's perfection.

"You're gorgeous," I mumbled, unable to stop myself. I glared at him as he laughed and kissed my nose.

"I'm glad you think so."

"I thought you weren't going to make love to me unless I begged you." I stared up at him with my body shivering. No part of our bodies was touching in that moment. But still, we were so close that I could feel his body hair against me, tickling me ever so lightly. It was pure torture being so close but not quite close enough.

"I'm not." He smiled evilly at me. "I'm going to make you beg me."

"Really?" I tried to smile at him seductively but was pretty sure my face just looked weird. "I think I'll have you begging me!"

"Oh?" He grinned and shifted slightly. I looked up at him in surprise and with raw lust as his hard cock pushed into my stomach. I reached down and grabbed it again, caressing it lightly before placing it lower. He gasped and his hands flew over my shoulders. He leaned into the wall as I slid his cock in between my legs and closed my thighs.

"I think you know what you want to do," I teased him.

"I do." He slid his cock back and forth slowly as he started to tease me and I moaned. The tip of his cock had somehow found my clit and he was grinding up and down on it. "But do you want me to do it?"

"You know I want you to." I looked up at him with begging eyes. I just wanted to feel him inside of me. I'd think about everything else tomorrow.

"You want me to what?" He smiled, pressing into me so that my breasts were crushed against his chest. He thrust his hips in a slow motion and his cock continued to slide in and out of my thighs, rubbing me and teasing me like crazy.

"You know." I groaned and closed my eyes. I tried to adjust my stance so that he would slide right into my aching spot.

"I know what?"

"Greyson," I groaned.

"Yes, Meg?" His voice was light, and I opened my eyes to see him smiling down at me.

"You're a pain," I mumbled, trying once again to adjust my body.

"But you still want me." His lips fell to my neck and he bit down hard into my skin. "You like this torture, don't you? You know that, when we finally make love, we are going to have the biggest explosion. I'm going to make you come like you've never come before."

"Go on then." I grabbed his waist and pulled him into me.

"Are you asking me to make love to you?" He looked down at me, and I felt the tip of his cock at my opening.

"Yes." I nodded excitedly. This was it. I was finally about to feel him inside of me.

"Not yet." He shook his head and pulled away from me. I froze, scared that he was about to leave me in the shower by myself. I knew in that moment that I would beg him to stay if he tried to leave. I'd get down on my knees and beg him for some relief before he left. I need him so badly at that moment. My entire body was craving his touch.

"Where are you going?" I whispered. I knew that my voice sounded weak, but I couldn't stop myself.

"Nowhere." He paused and stared at me. There wasn't much light in the room, but I could still see the look of wonder in his eyes.

"Oh," I spoke softly and we just stared at each other for a moment. I could feel my body shivering as we stood there, his expression closed.

"You're cold."

"Not really." I shook my head.

"Did you finish bathing?" he asked me softly and I shook my head.

"Good." He grabbed my bottle of body wash and squeezed some into his hands before stepping closer towards me. "I'll clean you, then."

"I don't need you to."

"But I want to."

His hands started rubbing my shoulders and then my arms, building up bubbles as the body wash met the water. His fingers were strong and rubbed me gently, scrubbing my skin with a light intensity as he bathed me. His fingers then fell to my breasts and he lathered them up slowly, twisting my nipples and pinching them as he caressed my breasts.

I leaned back against the wall excitedly, but then his fingers moved to my stomach and my back. He rubbed my back harder, massaging me as he cleaned me. I turned around then so he could have easier access to my back, and his fingers ran down along my spine to my buttocks, rubbing gently and cupping my butt cheeks in his hands. His fingers then slid around to my waist and he pulled me back towards him. I could feel his cock nestled between my butt cheeks as his fingers slid down farther until they were inside my legs, cleaning me delicately but thoroughly.

I pushed back into him as his fingers gently rubbed my clit. I could feel a small orgasm building and I knew that I was about to come. I groaned as his fingers left my private area and he bent down so he could rub down my thighs and calves. I jumped as I felt Greyson biting down on my butt, and he laughed and stood back up, grabbing me roughly and turning me around again.

"Your skin is so soft and supple. It feels like silk." His fingers traced the line along my collarbone and then down to my breasts. He cupped my breasts in his hands and held them gently, squeezing them and molding them into the palms of his hands. "They fit my hands perfectly." He stared at me with heavy eyes. "And they are so sweet." He leaned forward and took my left nipple into his mouth. "Oh, so sweet," he groaned as he sucked, his eyes still staring at me.

I stared back at him, unspeaking. There was nothing I could say. Nothing I wanted to say aside from, "Fuck me now."

"What?" He grinned at me and I realized that I had spoken out loud.

"Nothing!" I blushed.

"You want me as badly as I want you, don't you?"

"Why do you want me?" I whispered, needing to know what it was that had us like this.

"Because you're sexy as hell," he groaned and picked me up. "Wrap your legs around my waist." I did as he'd said and he pushed me back against the wall. "I'm going to fuck you now."

"You are?" I swallowed and closed my eyes. I was ready. A part of me felt like I had been waiting for this moment my entire life.

"I am." His hands pushed my butt up a little higher and he leaned forward to kiss me. "I'm so fucking hard and ready," he growled and stuck his tongue into my mouth at the same time as he entered me slowly.

"Ooh!" I moaned into his mouth as I felt the length of him easily slide into me. I groaned as he filled me up, and I felt a small orgasm rip through my body. My body shuddered against him as he grunted and pushed me harder against the wall.

"You're so fucking sexy," he whispered in my ear as his cock slid slammed in and out of me faster. "And you're so wet."

"We are in the shower," I tried to joke, but the last part of my words was incoherent as I cried out.

"Your pussy has been waiting for me," he muttered and turned the water off. "I'm sure you're still going to remain wet as fuck, even with the water off." I ignored him and ran my hands through his hair and down his neck as he entered me. "Your pussy was made for me," he grunted as he slid in and out. "Do you like the way my hard cock feels as I enter you?" he muttered into my head and I nodded. "You like it when I talk dirty, huh?"

He laughed and then kissed me again as he increased his pace even more.

Our bodies bounced back and forth together, and I felt another orgasm building up in me as he fucked me hard and fast. I wanted to scream as I felt myself building up to a huge climax. Greyson could sense how close I was to another orgasm and he alternated the speed of his cock from slow to fast. I closed my eyes as I concentrated on the feel of his cock as he slid in and out of me with such beautiful intensity that I thought I was going to cry.

Greyson was in mid-slide when we heard the door open and two girls walked into the room. We froze as they started talking.

"That's weird that the lights are off," one of the girls spoke, but I didn't recognize the voice.

"I wonder if everyone has gone to bed," the other voice said.

"I suppose so." The first girl sighed. "So I think I'm leaving tomorrow."

"What?" The other girl sounded surprised.

"I'm being sent away," the first girl spoke in hushed tones. "I'm not supposed to say anything, but Patsy told me this evening. She told me I'm special and I'd passed all of the tests in flying colors. She told me there was a special place for me. A special man that was going to take care of me."

"What does that mean?" The other girl sounded shocked, and I knew that my insides had frozen at her words.

"I'm not sure. But I guess that means I'm special to someone." She sounded excited, and I wanted to scream at her. I looked into Greyson's eyes and they looked back at me with nothing but an empty expression.

"I hope they find someone special for me," the other girl said wistfully.

"I'm sure they will. You're great, Jenn."

"I want a husband as well."

"I don't know if it's a husband waiting for me." The other girl's voice was low. "In fact, I think that—"

Greyson slammed his fist against the wall and a loud sound reverberated around the room. I heard the girls scream, and one of them cried out, "Is anyone in here?"

Greyson looked at me pointedly and I flushed, annoyed. "It's just me," I finally called back to them, and Greyson looked pleased.

"Oh, okay," the first girl called back, and I could hear obvious displeasure in her voice. "Are you alone?"

I paused for a second, wondering if I should say something. And then Greyson started moving inside of me again. My legs clenched around him and I leaned back against the wall, heart beating fast and mind already drifting to the pleasure he was about to give me again.

"Answer her," he commanded me as he pushed me back against the wall harder and slowly slid in and out of me. His hands pinned me back against the wall and he moved in so that my breasts were crushed against his chest. "Tell her," he whispered into my ear and increased his pace.

"Yeah," I gasped out. "I'm alone."

"Okay." Her voice sounded unsure. "We'll come back." I heard her whisper something to the other girl and I listened as they quickly walked toward the door. I wasn't sure why they were leaving already, especially since I had said it was only me.

"Why did you stop her from talking?" I looked into Greyson's eyes and held on to his back tightly.

"She had no business talking about what was happening to her." He looked angry. "I don't know what Patsy was thinking."

"What do you mean?" I gasped and then moaned as his hips started gyrating against me and he grabbed my ass, pulling me into him harder. I felt the weight of his hard cock nestled inside of me, working its way in and out as if he already knew every part of me.

The familiarity with which he treated me made me feel heady and it intensified the pleasure I was experiencing. Greyson was no fumbling lover, unsure of his actions. He was strong, powerful, and in complete control. The way he touched me in just the right spot and kissed me at just the right time. The way his fingers exerted pressure in just the right spots intensified the climax that was building up inside of me. My entire body quivered as his long, hard cock took control of my body.

Greyon's lips crushed down on mine and his tongue slid into my mouth, mimicking the movements of his cock down below. Our bodies were soapy and wet and the sensation in my nipples as they rubbed back and forth against his chest made my clutch him tighter. Every part of my body was tingling, and I didn't want the feeling to stop. My body wanted to become part of him. It wanted to mesh with his so that I could feel this pleasure forever.

But my brain was screaming at me to push him away. A part of me wanted to demand that he tell me what was going on. And a part of me was dying inside, even though another part of me was experiencing the most exquisite pleasure. I was experiencing the most intense pleasure and psychological pain that I'd ever felt at the same time, and I was starting to feel like I was having an out-of-body experience.

"Mind your own business, Meg," he groaned as he increased his pace. He was breathing heavily, and I knew that he was close to an orgasm.

"I don't want to mind my own business!" I screamed. "I want to know who I'm fucking!"

"You're fucking Greyson Twining," he grunted and his body shuddered against me as he climaxed.

I wrapped my legs around him tighter and felt myself joining him as an orgasm racked though my body. I gripped his shoulders as my body shook and he continued to fuck me hard as we both came.

A few seconds later, he fell against me, panting, and we stared at each other with stars in our eyes. I slowly unwrapped my legs from around his waist and he let me down to the ground. He turned on the water again and let it wash over us before picking up my body wash again.

"I guess it's time to wash our sins away." He poured some body wash into my hands and then started scrubbing down his own body. I rubbed my body gently, not looking at him and feeling slightly hurt at his words.

"What's your game, Greyson?" I whispered to him.

"You don't want to know, Meg." He shook his head, his eyes bleak. "I'm not a man you want to get to know."

"You can't just say that. That's not an answer." My voice rose, and I could feel myself getting angry. I was starting to feel slightly ashamed of myself for what I'd done. I needed to know what was really going on.

"It's done, Meg." He shook his head and looked away from me. "Leave it alone."

"Why is Brandon Hastings coming tomorrow?" I said the only thing I thought would get a reaction from him. Greyson didn't look surprised at my words. In fact, he seemed to expect what I was going to say.

"He's coming because he's a sinner." He shrugged and turned off the shower. "He's coming because he started the club with me. He's coming because we have business to take care of."

"What does that mean?" I looked at him with wide eyes.

"You don't want to know. You should go back to your room now." And with that, he stepped out of the stall, leaving me alone and vulnerable. I was no closer to knowing anything. All I knew now was that I was capable of making bad decisions. Very, very bad decisions.

CHAPTER FOUR

I walked back to my room in tears. I felt like a part of my soul had been torn out of my body. I decided to go back to the study to try to call Katie again. I needed to hear her voice. She was someone familiar and trustworthy, and I needed that right now. I felt like I was in a pit with snakes and dragons and I didn't know if either side was good.

I looked around to see if I was being followed this time. I thought it was strange that Greyson had seen me go into the study and hadn't asked me why I had gone in. It was also strange that he had come to find me and had been following me. He'd never said why.

I opened the door to the study slowly and walked in. What did it all mean? Why had Greyson come to find me? David had made it clear that I shouldn't expect to see Greyson until tomorrow. What did it mean that he had come to find me this evening?

I hurried to the desk and picked up the phone. I dialed the numbers quickly and held my breath. I wasn't sure if I'd be able to get through the night without sobbing my eyes out if I didn't get to talk to Katie.

"Hello?" Her voice sounded tired, but I didn't care.

"It's me," I whispered into the phone.

"Meg!" she screeched, and my heart warmed as I smiled. How I loved Katie! She was more than my best friend—she was like my sister. "What is going on? Where are you?"

"I'm still at the club." I spoke into the phone softly and looked around the room, paranoid that someone was spying on me somehow.

"Why are you whispering?" She sounded concerned. "What's wrong?"

"Nothing. Look, I need to ask you something. Where is Brandon?"

"Brandon, honey. Meg's on the phone!" Katie sounded loved up as she whispered to Brandon, and I wanted to shout at her. I heard him saying something to her, but I couldn't quite hear what he was saying.

"Katie!" I said her name, loudly this time.

"Yes, Meg?" This time, she sounded confused.

"Can you get away from Brandon for a moment?"

"Yeah? Why?"

"I need to talk to you. And I need to make sure that Brandon isn't around."

"Oh my God, what's going on?" Katie sounded slightly panicked. "Hold on, Meg. Brandon, I need to talk to her first."

"What's going on, Katie?"

"Brandon, she needs to tell me something." Katie's voice was sharp, and I could hear something akin to fear in her tone. "What's it about, Meg?"

"Katie, I told you I didn't want Brandon to know."

"We don't have secrets." Katie's voice was petulant, and I wanted to scream. She hadn't seen the man in seven years and already she was taking his side over mine.

"Tell him I know about his 'college fiancée' Maria," I spouted out.

"Maria?" Katie sounded confused. "How did you hear about that?"

"You know about Maria?" It was my turn to be confused.

"Didn't I tell you? He was only dating her because her dad used to work for him. I told you that Maria and Matt and Will are all related, right?"

"Wait, what? Are you talking about the new Maria or his college fiancée Maria?"

"Why would I be talking about his college fiancée?" Katie sounded confused, and then I heard her gasp.

"Meg." Brandon's voice was smooth and firm as he spoke into the phone. "Are you okay?"

"I'm fine."

"How are you making this call?"

"What are you talking about?" I feigned ignorance.

"You need to leave the club right now, Meg. I told you that you shouldn't be there."

"How did you know that, Brandon?"

"What do you mean?"

"Does Katie know that you started the club?"

He was silent on the other side so I continued.

"Does Katie know the truth about Maria? Does she even know that you're planning on coming here tomorrow?"

"Meg, you don't understand," he pleaded. "Please."

"Please what?" I screeched. "You and Greyson are freaks."

"You don't understand." He sighed. "Greyson isn't like most men."

"What does that mean?" I sat down on the chair. I couldn't stop myself from gripping the phone tightly. I wanted to know more about Greyson, even if it was from Brandon.

"What is going on, Brandon?" Katie's voice was loud and she sounded angry. I knew that she had finally figured out that there was more going on here than met the eye.

"Meg, I have to tell you that, whatever you heard, it wasn't my fault. I didn't know." His voice was bleak.

"But you lied about—"

"We were both heartbroken when she died," he whispered and then the phone disconnected.

I sat there feeling numb and whispered into the dead phone, "But you lied about dating Maria in college."

It was obvious to me now that Brandon had snatched the phone from Katie because he'd been worried about a much bigger problem. Maria was dead? And was his Maria also Nancy's Maria? How had she died? What role had Greyson and Brandon played in her death? My mind was bursting with questions and for the first time, I was scared. Really and truly scared.

I didn't want to leave the study to go back to the room. I didn't want to see Nancy or David. I didn't want to see Frank and Elizabeth. And most of all, I didn't want to see Greyson.

My heart ached as I thought about him and the way I had given myself to him so easily. At the time, it had seemed natural. Our attraction was great, but a part of me had thought that there was something else there. Some deeper magnetism that couldn't be explained but had been felt as soon as we'd met.

But I knew I was fooling myself. Greyson was just a sexy older man who had filled me with lust, and I had succumbed like a two-bit whore.

I jumped up and put the phone back on its charger. "Stop it, Meg," I muttered angrily at myself. I hated it when I grew self-deprecating, which I was prone to do when things didn't go well in my life. I was not going to allow myself to feel cheap just because I had slept with Greyson Twining. I was a woman, a twenty-first-century woman, and if I wanted to sleep with a man because his very glance made my panties wet, then I wasn't going to ridicule or beat myself up for it. I could be my own worst enemy sometimes.

I exited the room and looked down the corridor before deciding which way to go. I wasn't sure if I should try to explore what was going on or if I should just go back to the room.

I decided to head back to the room as I was feeling tired and depressed. I needed a good night's sleep so that I would be refreshed in the morning. I needed to know why Brandon was coming to the club. I prayed to God that Katie was questioning him about whatever suspicions she had. I only wished that I had been able to speak to her for a little bit longer before Brandon had taken the phone.

I turned the corner, walked to the room, and was surprised to see the door open.

"Don't make me look like a fool again." David's voice was loud and angry as he spoke, and I froze.

"Leave her alone, David." Nancy's voice was urgent. "She's nice."

"She can help us." David's tone was lower now. "If we want to get them, we can do it through her. She's our best shot. We can finally get justice."

"I don't know." Nancy sounded worried. "I just think that—"

"What they did." David's voice broke. "Justice has to be served for what they are doing to these women."

"But ..." Nancy said something else, but I couldn't hear.

I quickly backed away from the room since I didn't want them to know that I knew David had gone back to the room. So I'd been correct: David knew Nancy. And I could tell that they were very well acquainted.

I tried to think about the other facts I knew. Elizabeth seemed to know Frank, and Nancy had said something about Frank as well. So maybe all four of them knew each other. But it didn't really add up. And who were the two guys I'd seen in the hallway? I was now thinking I'd seen Frank and David talking. That would make the most sense. But then, who were they talking about? Nothing was adding up. Was Frank also an undercover cop, then?

I rounded a corner and heard some music playing from a room at the end of the corridor. It sounded like an old Edith

Piaf record my uncle used to play when I was growing up, and I walked toward the music to see what was going on.

This was a part of the club I'd not been in before. It seemed more residential and homey. There was no office or dorm feel to this section, and I suddenly felt uneasy. This was a part of the club I was pretty sure I wasn't supposed to be in.

I pressed my ear against the door to see if I was correct in my musical guess and almost jumped a mile when the door opened.

"Hello, Meg." He looked at me with darkened eyes and a short smile.

"Greyson."

"Came to beg me for some more?"

"Some more what?" I asked dumbly, staring into his vivid blue eyes.

"You know what!" He looked me over and ushered me into the room. "Want to come in?"

"I was going to my room." I shook my head and mumbled. "Sorry to disturb you."

"Your room is nowhere near here. How'd you wind up down this corridor?"

"I thought I had someone playing Edith Piaf."

"You listen to French music?" He looked at me in surprise.

"Not really. But I did growing up. My uncle used to play her records a lot."

"That makes me feel old."

"You're not old."

"I'm too old for you."

"Is that something you've been thinking about?" I asked hopefully, allowing my emotions to get caught up again. Maybe this was something special and out of the ordinary for him as well.

"Not really."

"Oh." Disappointment filled me, and once again I felt like a bit of a fool. That emotion was becoming too familiar to me, and I hoped that it wasn't going to continue.

"Come in for a bit and have a drink."

"I thought we weren't allowed to have alcohol."

"Most of the girls aren't." He nodded. "But you're a special case."

"I am?"

"You know that already."

"Why, because we ..." My voice cut off. I couldn't bring myself to say "fucked," and I knew that what we had done couldn't be considered making love.

"Come in and have a seat." He grabbed my hand and pulled me into the room.

I looked around eagerly and was surprised to find myself in a room that resembled a comfortable living room.

"Do you live here?"

"Sometimes." He smiled and pointed me towards the couch. "It's not my only home, but I spend many nights here."

"It's nice." I sat down on the couch. "This is really comfortable."

"Isn't it?" He laughed and sat down next to me. "Can I get you a drink?"

"No, thanks." I shook my head and watched as he picked up a glass off of the table and took a sip.

"Want some?" He handed me his glass and I shook my head. "It will warm you up. I know how easily you can shiver."

"I'm quite warm as it is, thank you."

"Are you always this combative?"

"I'm not combative." And then I laughed. "Well, not normally."

"Have a sip of whiskey." He tried to hand me his glass again, and I sighed.

"This is peer pressure, you know." I made a face as I took the glass and sniffed it. "I don't really like whiskey."

"That's not surprising. It's more of a man's drink." He smiled. "Now drink."

"Are you trying to get me drunk, Mr. Twining?"

"I don't think I need to." He looked into my eyes then and gave me a small smile.

I shivered at the truth of his words. He was right, of course. He did not need to get me drunk in order to have his way with me. Shoot, at this point, all he needed to do was touch me and I would become putty in his hands.

"So you like Edith?" I questioned him, changing the subject.

"I do." He nodded and leaned back into the couch. "My mother was French."

"Oh, cool." I thought for a moment. "Did she pass away?"

"Yes, when I was young."

"I'm sorry."

"Don't be. It's not your fault." He shrugged.

"Still, it must have been hard to lose your mother when you were young."

"Is that code for 'That's a possible reason why you're fucked up, Greyson'?"

"No, no." I shook my head. "Of course not."

"I was going to say that you're probably right." His eyes glittered at me and he moved closer to me on the couch and took a large sip of his whiskey. "My life was never the same after my mother died."

"Why not?"

"Because my father was never the same." He stared at the Persian rug underneath his coffee table. "My father always had so much money and power. He thought he was invincible. And then the love of his love died of cancer and there was nothing he could do. His money and his power meant nothing to those cancer cells. My mom was diagnosed with breast cancer and died within three months." His voice grew thoughtful. "In a way, I suppose that affected me more than I thought. I saw the devastation that my father went through, that he still lives."

"He never got over your mother?"

"He loved her too much." He sighed. "But he also never got over the fact that he couldn't do anything. He's a bloody titan, but he couldn't do a damn thing to stop the cancer from spreading."

"It sounds like she must have been pretty far along if she passed away so quickly." I looked at him and he nodded.

"Cancer's a bitch." He spoke the words with such contempt that part of me wanted to laugh, but I knew it wasn't a laughing matter.

"What was your life like after your mother died?"

"I was sent to boarding school." He shrugged. "I didn't mind. It was fun, and I met Brandon."

"I didn't know he went to boarding school." I looked at him in surprise. "I thought you knew each other from college."

"Well, we did know each other in college." He shrugged nonchalantly. "But we knew each other in high school, as well. Brandon was always my best friend."

"Are you still best friends?"

"No." He shook his head and his eyes looked at me with a pained expression. "No, we're not."

"Brandon is an asshole, huh?" I looked at him with a pleading expression. "Please tell me the truth. My best friend is dating him again. He really hurt her a lot the first time. I want to make sure that doesn't happen again."

"Brandon's not the worst guy." His eyes were bleak. "Let's just say I'm the devil and he was my apprentice."

"What do you guys do here?" I almost begged him to tell me. I just needed to hear the truth from his mouth. I wanted to understand how they could have gotten into this business.

"We have a strip club." He paused for a second, and his eyes were light as he looked at me. His hand fell to my leg and he started squeezing my knee. "I thought that was obvious."

"So we're all training to be strippers?" I raised an eyebrow. I knew my face was turning red because I could feel the heat in my cheeks. I was angry. Really, really angry. I knew this was much more than a strip club.

"No." He shook his head.

"So the girls who aren't strippers are going to be …?" I continued, ignoring the lust building up in me as Greyson's hand flew to my thigh.

"Why is this so important to you?" Greyson sighed and leaned in towards me. "You don't want to know, Meg."

"Or do you mean you don't want me to know?" I pulled away from him. His eyes were a mere two inches from mine, and I could feel the heat of his breath on my lips as he spoke.

"I mean that it's not important. What's important is what we have."

"What are you talking about?" I whispered.

"The hot sex." His tongue licked my lips. "I've never been so attracted to a woman before. Never thought about and wanted a woman so badly."

"Well, you've had me already."

"I want you again."

His lips pressed against mine softly and he kissed me with such a gentle sweetness that I found myself gravitating towards him. Our lips and tongues explored each other, both of us looking for answers in the depths of each other's mouths. "I've never met a girl like you before, Meg." He sat back after a few minutes with a dazed look in his eyes.

"What do you mean?" I asked, trying not to blush.

"I'm forty-two and I've never met a woman who was as beautiful, honest, fearless, and intelligent as you." He frowned and jumped up. "You're messing up my mind," he muttered as he walked to a wet bar. He picked up a decanter and poured some more whiskey into his glass. "Would you like a drink?"

"I don't do hard stuff."

"I've got chasers."

"I'll have a tequila sunrise if you have the ingredients."

"Let me see… Tequila, check. Orange juice, check. And grenadine, check." He smiled at me. "Would you like a cherry on top as well?"

"Yes, please." I nodded eagerly and he laughed.

"Sometimes, I look at you and I can't believe you're only twenty-five because you seem so much wiser that that. But other times, when you're excited or petulant, you remind me of a little child, and I'm left wondering if you could really be twenty-five." He walked back towards me with our drinks in his hands.

"So you're saying that I remind you of someone much older and much younger at the same time?"

"I guess so."

"I'm not sure that's a compliment."

"Good. I didn't intend it to be a compliment." He handed me my drink and sat down.

"Oh, well, that makes it all better." I shook my head and laughed. "I'm not sure what the point of your little talk was then."

"Just to tell you that you confuse me."

"How can I be confusing you if you don't even know me?"

"You're confusing my thoughts," he muttered. "Or maybe I should say complicating them."

"How am I complicating your thoughts?"

"Meg, you have far too many questions." He placed his glass down on the table. "Now, tell me something about you."

"What do you want to know?"

"Everything." His tone was light, but he looked serious.

"Why?" I stared at him with bated breath.

"I don't know." He looked at me with an expression I couldn't place. "I really don't know."

"That's helpful." I laughed, but I felt light inside. "Um, let's see. I went to Columbia for undergrad."

"No, no." He grinned and moved closer to me again. "I don't want to know what's on your resume. Tell me something about you that no one else knows."

"I don't know." I made a face and sipped some of my drink. It went down my throat smoothly and I was instantly warmed inside.

"What's the craziest sexual experience you've ever had?"

"You really want to know?"

"Yes." He nodded.

"Today. Tonight with you," I said honestly. "Nothing else comes close."

"In more ways than one, I hope."

"No comment." I grinned back at him.

"Okay, what's the next one?" He shifted closer to me on the couch.

"I mean, it wasn't crazy, but when I was in high school, I had a boyfriend and we had sex on his couch once under a blanket."

"What's so crazy about that?"

"His dad was sitting in a chair in the room with us." I laughed, and Greyson joined in.

"Okay, that's pretty risqué."

"What about you?" I asked curiously.

"I've got so many, I wouldn't know where to start."

"That's not fair," I protested.

"Life's not fair." He laughed and leaned forward to kiss my neck.

"Tell me, Greyson." I moaned slightly as he bit down hard. "You're going to leave a mark."

"I know." He laughed and then kissed along my neck to my lips. "I don't think you want to know my craziest."

"I do." I nodded.

He sat back and grinned. "When I was in college, I used to date this girl. Or rather, we used to fuck. I don't date. One night, I slipped into her dorm room to have sex. I got into the bed and kissed her, and she moaned against me and whispered my name, telling me how glad she was that I was there."

"What's so crazy about that?" I shrugged, feeling slightly jealous.

"It had been dark when I got into the room," he continued. "So anyways, we start having sex and her roommate comes into the room and turns on the light."

"Oh, let me guess. You guys had a threesome?" I interjected.

He shook his head and placed a finger on my lips before grinning. "No, we didn't have a threesome. The girl turns on the light and starts screaming."

"Oh no, why?"

"Shh." He laughs. "So I look up and see the girl I thought I was fucking standing at the door. Beneath me, I see her roommate grinning up at me and clutching my hips."

"Oh, my God." My eyes widened. "That's crazy. What did you do?"

"What do you mean what did I do? I kept fucking until I came and then I left."

"You kept fucking?" My mouth dropped open in shock. "Even after you realized you were with the wrong girl?"

He nodded at me and bit down on my lower lip hard. "I already told you before, Meg. I'm no angel."

"But what about the girl you were seeing. What did she do?"

"I have no idea." He shrugged. "After she stopped screaming, I continued doing what I was doing."

"You really don't seem to care about women's feelings, do you?" A part of me felt sad.

"I wouldn't say that."

"I guess maybe your mother's death really affected you. Maybe you were so hurt by your mother dying and your father withdrawing into himself that you vowed to never fall in love."

"What are you? A shrink?" He rolled his eyes. "I enjoy my life, Meg. I'm not looking to hurt anyone, but I'm also not looking to fall in love."

"So you just go from bed to bed and from fuck to fuck and you don't care who it's with?"

"Of course I care."

"It doesn't seem that way." I pulled away from him, angry at myself. I jumped up off the couch. "Look, I have to go. I should get to bed."

"I never lied to you, Meg." He jumped up as well.

"I never said you did." I tried to walk past him, but he reached out and stopped me.

"I want you to spend the night with me."

"I don't want to," I lied, trying to push past him.

"Liar." He pulled me towards him. "You want me as badly as I want you."

"You're so full of yourself."

"Deny it then."

"Why would I deny it? You obviously know that you can have any woman who you want. It doesn't mean anything." I shrugged.

"I don't want just any woman. I want you."

"Am I supposed to feel special? Woohoo, I'm your flavor of the day."

"Brandon and I wanted to rule the world." His eyes glittered into mine as he changed the subject. "We wanted to be omnipotent."

"Why?"

"Why do boys generally want to rule the world?"

"I don't think you're like most guys."

"I'm not better than them."

"I don't think you're better, either."

And then he laughed and shook his head. "So honest, Meg."

"I wish you were as honest."

"I've never lied to you."

"But you're not telling me everything."

"I don't have to tell you anything."

"Put me in my place, why don't you?"

"I'm not perfect, Meg. I'm forty-two years old and I've lived a life driven by the pursuit of not caring."

"How can you be driven by not caring? Most men are after money or power or women or whatever."

"I had money. Money brings power, and well, women have never been a problem for me."

"Because you're so handsome, right?" I rolled my eyes.

"I can't help it if women find me sexually attractive."

"Give me a break."

"I also can't help it if I find you sexually attractive." His fingers stroked my cheek.

"I'm not that girl, Greyson. I know, I know. I've acted like that girl, but that's not me." I took a deep breath. "I'm not comfortable here." I mumbled the words, scared to see his reaction. "There's too much going on. I think I want to leave."

"What are you scared of?"

"I'm scared of the things I'm hearing. I'm scared that you really are the devil. I'm scared I'm going to lose myself and my perception of good and evil."

"Do you think I'm evil?"

"I don't know," I answered honestly. All signs pointed to yes, but I didn't want to believe that he was capable of such evil. I didn't want to believe that I could be so attracted to and consumed with someone who was pure evil. I'd always prided myself on my common sense and ability to see who people were when I first met them. My people radar had never been off before, but I had never had this sort of attraction to a man before.

"I suppose that's better than a yes." He gave me a wry smile. "Will you stay?"

"Why do you want me to stay?"

"I don't know."

"Neither of us seems to know a thing," I sighed and he wrapped his arms around me.

"Dance with me."

"What?" I made a face. "Really?"

"Not dance for me, dance with me."

"I'm not much of a dancer."

"You don't have to be much of a dancer." He grabbed my hands and spun me around. "You just have to move."

"We're going to dance to 'La Vie En Rose'?"

"Why not?" He smiled, put his arm around my waist, and started humming. We spun around the room and I tried to match his footsteps and not step on his feet as we waltzed. "Da da da da da da, da da, da da, *la vie en rose*," he hummed and sang, and I smiled up at him as we glided together. We started laughing as we nearly hit the coffee table and I fell against him in my quick attempt to avoid his feet.

"Sorry. I told you I sucked."

"No, you don't." His eyes were full of mirth, and we continued dancing in silence, only the music and his humming filling the room.

"You're a good dancer," I finally spoke after the song had finished.

"I used to dance with my mom." His smiled. "She wanted me to be a ballroom dancer."

"She what?" I looked up at him in surprise and he laughed.

"There are many things you don't know about me."

"But now I do. Well, I know some. You wanted to be a comedian and your dad said no, and your mom wanted you to be a ballroom dancer."

"Which I never wanted, by the way." He laughed. "I absolutely hated dancing with my mom every week. Now, of course, I'm glad she made me. I'll always carry those memories with me."

"Was she a good dancer then?"

"The best," he said simply, and then he held his hand out and twirled me around and around. "She was a ballet dancer when she was younger. In fact, that's how my father met her."

"Oh?"

"His girlfriend dragged him to the ballet." He laughed. "My father saw my mom on the stage and she captivated him. He fell in love with her as he watched her dance."

"Wow."

"It was *The Nutcracker* as well. Not clichéd at all." He smiled, and I could hear nostalgia in his voice.

"So how did he meet her?"

"He went back to the ballet the next day. In fact, he went back to fifty-nine performances and then he went backstage and talked to her."

"And what did she say?"

"She ignored him." He laughed. "Well, she thanked him for the flowers he had brought and dismissed him."

"Oh no." I felt my heart thudding. "That's sad."

"The story has a happy ending, Meg. I do exist, remember?" He laughed. "He went back to the ballet for three more months and every other week he went backstage and took her flowers. He didn't go every day because he didn't want her to think he was a creep."

"And what happened?"

"One day he went back and she was crying." He looked away from me then. "And he took her into his arms and let her cry. After about ten minutes, she stopped and they went out for watee."

"Watee? Huh?"

"That's what they called it. She had water and he had coffee."

"Oh, that's cute."

"Yeah. They went out for watee for the next two weeks and then my father proposed."

"What?"

"Yeah." He laughed. "He knew from the first night that she was the one."

"That's so romantic," I sighed wistfully. Why couldn't Greyson be like his dad?

"I'm sure you're wondering what happened to me," he laughed, and I blushed at how clearly he had been able to read my thoughts.

"Well …"

"It's okay." He pulled me back to the couch with him. "Sometimes I wonder what happened to me as well."

"I've never heard a man say that before."

"As you get older, you begin to wonder what you've done with your life. Who you've hurt. Who you've helped. If the bad outweighs the good. If the good can ever outweigh the bad." His tone was deep as he pulled me onto his lap. "And then sometimes you just want to lose yourself and forget it all."

"Can you?"

"Forget it all?"

"Yeah."

"No. Never." He pulled my head down to his. "And in moments like this, I never want to forget."

I wrapped my arms around his head as he kissed me and I melted into him. I knew what he meant. This moment would stick with me forever and I never wanted to forget it. Even if I found out he was as bad as I thought he was. In this moment, he was wonderful. He was my dream guy. This was a perfect moment. A snapshot moment. It was one I would come back to in my mind and my dreams for years to come.

Greyson smelled divine, and I felt myself losing myself in him as we kissed. When his lips were on mine and his hands were on me, there was nothing more important to me than being with him.

"Oh, Meg," Greyson groaned as I massaged the top of his head and pulled the tips of his hair. He pushed me back down on the couch roughly and positioned his body on top of mine. I stared up at him and he smiled sweetly down at me, so sweetly that I thought my heart was going to break. "Stay the night, Meg."

"I don't want to," I lied.

"Tonight we'll just sleep. I just want to sleep with you." He kissed me lightly and leaned his chest down so that he was lightly touching my breasts without crushing me.

"I don't know."

"Don't think about it." His eyes pleaded with me. "Tonight, let's just enjoy that we got to meet. For tomorrow may be another story."

"What do you mean?" I frowned.

"Let's just enjoy this moment, please," he whispered in my ear. "It may be the one perfect moment we both have."

"Okay." I nodded up at him and wrapped my arms around his back to pull him down towards me closer. "Let's just enjoy tonight."

"And you never know." Greyson looked wistfully at me. "Tomorrow may never come."

CHAPTER FIVE

"You don't have to stop," I whispered back to Greyson as his fingers played with my belly button and stopped at the top of my pants. I backed my ass into him and he groaned as I grinded my ass into his stiffening cock.

"Meg." He held me close. "I just want to spoon."

"No, you don't," I giggled, feeling slightly drunk as I continued wiggling against him.

"You know me well," he growled as his hands reached up under my T-shirt and cupped my breasts. "I could spend the rest of my days losing myself in your body."

"Ooh," I moaned as his fingers slipped under my bra and pinched my nipples.

"Moan for me some more," he growled into my ear. "You turn me on so much when you moan."

"Oh, really?" I twisted my head and smiled at him before reaching back to see how much I had turned him on.

"See?" He grinned as I squeezed his hardness.

"Yes." I grinned back.

"I'm so hard for you," he groaned as his hands squeezed my breasts. "If I close my eyes, I can feel your pussy lips closing in on my cock, so tight and wet." He bit down on my neck. "Fuck, I want to take you again so badly."

"You can."

"No." He shook his head. "Tonight has been special. I don't want you to think it was about more than us just being together. I don't want you to think that tonight was about sex."

"But you don't want more than that?" I was hoping he would provide an answer that would make the night even more perfect.

"When my mother died, my father didn't leave the house for a month. Then he brought a different whore home every month. I'm not sure I ever saw him laugh again or really smile a genuine smile. I don't think he's ever truly enjoyed a full day since she's been gone." His voice was sad. "I never want my life to be like that. I never want to grow so close to someone that losing them will break me. I never want to love. I never want more than I'm willing to give."

"I see." My heart broke for Greyson and his father.

"So the answer to your question is that, yes, tonight is about more than sex, but no, I don't want more than that." He sighed. "I know that doesn't make sense. It seems that age doesn't make us wiser in some ways. It doesn't make what I'm saying sound any less confusing."

"I understand what you're saying. You've been hurt." I bit down on my lower lip. "It's understandable."

"I'm not a broken boy, Meg." His fingers slipped back down my stomach and he undid the top of my pants. "You can't fix me. Please don't go making that mistake. Many women's hearts have been broken, thinking they can fix me. I'm a man. And I'm never going to change."

"I would never try to—" I gasped aloud as his fingers slipped into my panties. "I thought we weren't going to—" I gasped again as I felt his fingers rubbing roughly against my clit. "Greyson," I moaned, my body bucking into him.

"I said no sex. That doesn't mean I can't make you come." He laughed, and I closed my eyes, allowing the sensations of pleasure to occupy my mind. "In fact, I would love to make you come all night long."

"How are you going to do that?" I whispered.

"With my fingers and with my tongue." He laughed gently and increased the pressure of his fingers against me. I felt an orgasm already building up inside of me, and I knew that tonight was definitely going to be one of the best nights of my life.

***

"Meg? Meg, wake up." Nancy's voice sounded anxious. "You have to go and shower now. Or you're going to be late."

"Huh?" I yawned and stretched. I looked around the room in confusion. I had no idea how I'd gotten into my own room. The last thing I remembered was being on the couch with Greyson.

"Wake up. You have ten minutes to shower and get ready. We don't want to be late again."

"I, uh, sure. I won't shower." I jumped out of bed. "Do you know what time I got back to the room last night?" I asked casually.

"No." Nancy shook her head. "I didn't hear you come in at all."

"Oh."

"But I fell asleep early."

"Did you talk to anyone last night?" I bent down and scratched my foot.

"No. After you left, I just went to sleep."

"Oh, okay. No one came looking for me or anything?"

"No."

"Okay." I stood up again and looked at her face. She looked tired, and I wondered what secrets she was hiding. "It's crazy that David is an undercover cop, though, right?"

"I guess so." She looked away from me.

"He can really help you," I continued, pushing the topic.

"I guess so."

"He said that he thinks there might be some sort of trafficking going on. Though I'm not sure if this is what it's called." I sighed. "But he said women are being sent to be some sort of prostitutes to rich men," I continued, trying to push it to see what she would say. "Do you think that's what happened to Maria? Maybe she's somewhere in another country?"

"No." Nancy shook her head. "She's not in another country."

"How do you know?"

"I just know." She walked over to me and looked around. "Be careful, Meg. People aren't who they seem to be."

"What do you mean?"

"Just be careful who you're falling for." She bit her lip. "I don't want to see something bad happen to you."

"Why would something bad happen to me?"

"You're getting too close, Meg." Her eyes were wide. "He's not going to fall in love with you. He's not who he seems to be. He still loves her."

A loud noise made us both jump, and Nancy backed away from me quickly.

"Are you okay, Nancy? What more do you know?" I pressed on, hoping she would just tell me everything she knew.

"I'll see you outside." Her face was white. "This was a mistake to come here. I don't know what I was thinking."

"You wanted to find out what happened to Maria, didn't you?"

She looked at me and shrugged.

"Nancy, look, I trust you. I know you're not telling me everything, but I trust you. I found out something yesterday. There's a Maria that died. I don't know if she's your Maria, though."

Nancy's eyes widened and she froze. "You know too much."

"Nancy, we need to find out."

"Please, Meg. Just forget about it. Let's leave it."

"We can't just forget it, Nancy."

"I'll see you outside." Nancy gave me one last glance and ran out of the room.

I stood there looking at the door and my heart wouldn't stop racing. I was worried about Nancy. She seemed like she was going to crack any second now.

And I was still confused as to how I had gotten to the room. Had Greyson drugged me? I closed my eyes and tried to remember the previous night. I remembered us kissing and him spooning me on the couch. I remembered closing my eyes to enjoy the sensations a little bit more intensely, and then the next thing I remembered was waking up in this room.

I looked at the clock on the wall and realized I had two minutes to get outside. I ran out of the room quickly and towards the courtyard. I was going to have another talk with Nancy as soon as Patsy was done with us. I needed her to trust me and I needed her to tell me what was going on.

I hurried into the courtyard and saw Elizabeth and her minions laughing at me again. I ignored them and looked around for Nancy but I couldn't see her anywhere. I stood to the side and waited for her to come out. Maybe she'd had to go to the bathroom first?

The panic started when Patsy walked out with David, Frank, and Bruno. Nancy still wasn't out in the courtyard as of yet and I knew that she wouldn't have been late. There was no way she would have been late. She had wanted us both to be on time this morning.

"Good morning, everyone." Patsy looked at us all with a grim face. "There have been some changes to the program today."

"Oh, no more tests?" Elizabeth spoke up, and her friends giggled.

"Today, some of the girls will be leaving us," Patsy continued and my heart stopped. Already?

"Excuse me. My roommate isn't here." It was my turn to interrupt. "I'm not sure where she is."

"Who's your roommate?" David looked at me blankly, but I could see worry in his eyes.

"Her name is Nancy."

"Nancy is gone." Patsy gave me a quick glance and turned to David. "You can mark her off of your list."

I spoke up again. "But I just saw her."

"She's gone."

What could have happened to her? Had Greyson done something? I knew I was feeling paranoid, but I couldn't stop myself from worrying. Where was Nancy? I looked around, and I could see that Elizabeth was staring at me. We made eye contact and she looked like she was worried as well. I frowned at her and she shook her head slightly. I didn't understand what she was trying to communicate to me, and I turned away from her.

"Excuse me. I have to go to the restroom," I called out before leaving the courtyard. I saw Patsy give me an angry glance, but I didn't let that stop me from running back into the building. Enough was enough. I needed to start getting some answers.

I ran through the hallways until I came to Greyson's living room. I pushed open the door to confront him, but the room was empty. I looked around the room and thought about the night before and how wonderful it had been. He'd really opened up to me. I felt like I was getting to know two different Greysons. One was gentle, kind, sweet, and slightly broken, and the other one was slightly nefarious and exuded an evil danger that I couldn't even comprehend. The problem was my whole body was telling me that he wasn't that evil man. Though Nancy had just warned me about him before she'd disappeared. She'd seemed so worried and scared for me.

I walked out of the room slowly and thought, *If Greyson isn't in here, where else would he be?* That's when it hit me. He would be in his office. He had to be in the office.

I ran back to my room to make sure Nancy wasn't there again and was about to run back out when I saw a piece of paper on my bed. I picked it up and read it quickly.

"First Maria, now Nancy. Who's next? Is it you, Meg?"

I stared at the paper for a few minutes and my face went white. Was the writer of the note trying to say that Nancy was dead? Or was he trying to say that Nancy had disappeared? Either way, I knew that enough time hadn't passed for her to just disappear or even be killed. Maybe the note was acting as a threat or scare tactic. Maybe the writer of the note was trying to warn me off of trying to find out.

I placed the note in my pocket and ran the hallway, trying to remember my way back to Greyson's office. I knew I was close when I got to the dark grey hallway that I had waited in on the day I'd arrived. Only this time I didn't patiently wait outside. I burst into the room and thanked God when I saw Greyson sitting at his desk.

"Missed me, did you?" He smirked, and I tried not to succumb to his snarky charm.

"Where's Nancy?"

"Who?" He blinked. "Oh, your roommate?"

"Yes, my roommate as you well know!" I shouted and banged my fists on the table. "Where is she?"

"Why would I know where she is?" He frowned and stood up. "What's wrong, Meg?"

"She's gone."

"Is this about me putting you back in your own bed last night?" He stroked my hair. "I thought it would be better for all involved if you woke up in your own room."

"I don't care about that."

"I missed you in my arms when I woke up. I felt oddly bereft."

"Sure you did." This time, I did roll my eyes.

"I did." He hugged me. "Are you sure your roommate isn't in the courtyard?"

"I was there and she's gone. Patsy said she left."

"Maybe she just left then. We don't hold anyone against their will."

"Patsy said stuff is changing today." I changed the subject. "People are leaving. Was Nancy one of the girls you had down on the list to leave?"

"No." Greyson's eyes darkened.

"What plans have changed?" I pushed my luck, hoping to get a real answer.

"Yes, there's been a change of plans." His eyes seemed to look right through me. "But the actual change of plans is none of your concern."

"I want to know what happened to Nancy. Where is she?"

"Meg, I have no idea what happened to her."

"She warned me about you this morning and now she's gone." I pushed against him. "I don't believe it's coincidence."

"Meg, I swear to God. I have no idea who this girl is or why she would be warning you off of me."

"She's Maria's sister!" I shot out and looked to see his reaction.

He backed away from me then and his eyes changed. I knew instantly that he was shocked at the news. He hadn't known that Nancy and Maria were related. And if he hadn't known that, then what threat would she have been to him? No, he wasn't responsible for Nancy's disappearance or running away.

"Maria?"

"Don't pretend to be ignorant, Greyson. Not now." I sighed. "Please."

"I like you, Meg." He grabbed my shoulders. "But there are things you don't want to know. Things you don't need to know. Please do not push this."

"Greyson." My voice cracked as I said his name. We stared at each other for a few minutes and then tears started falling from my eyes. "I can't take this anymore."

"What are you saying?" His fingers wiped the tears off of my face gently.

"I'm saying I want to leave as well."

"I thought you needed a job."

"I'll move to a different apartment. Shit, I'll move home and live with my parents." I shrugged. "I'm tired, I can't deal with this anymore."

"I don't know what you think you know, Meg." He shook his head. "But please don't leave. Not yet."

"Why do you want me to stay?"

"I'm not as bad as you think I am, Meg." He sighed. "I know I warned you away, but my bite isn't as bad as my bark."

"Wouldn't every wolf say that?" I shook my head and looked around his office. I saw some photos on the wall in the corner and walked over to look at them. "Is that you and Brandon Hastings?" I stared at the photos searchingly, hoping to find some clues.

"Yes." He nodded and his eyes were clouded. I was about to ask him another question when Patsy burst into the office panting.

"Mr. Twining." Patsy ran into the office out of breath. "Two of the girls are refusing to go. I told them that they had to."

"Patsy." Greyson held his hand up to stop her, but she continued on with her speech.

"There's a baby." Her face looked worried. "I'm sorry. I forgot to check. But she's having a baby. Her people won't accept girls with babies."

"Then send her to someone who will." Greyson shrugged and looked over at me in the corner with a blank expression. My face had grown ashen and I thought I was going to faint. "Patsy, I am confident you can take care of this, right?"

"Yes, Mr. Twining." Patsy nodded. "I know what to do. I know who will take women with babies."

"Good." Greyson nodded and watched as Patsy walked out of the door. "There's no need to hide in the corner, Meg."

"So it's true then?" I gulped out, barely able to talk.

"What's true?"

"You do send girls away?"

"I," he started and sighed. "I don't know what to say." He looked back at me, and I was about to respond when someone else did for me.

"Maybe it's time to tell her the truth." Brandon's voice filled the room, and I turned to look at him, in shock and unable to believe that he was finally here in the flesh. "Maybe, it's time for us to acknowledge everything, Greyson."

"I don't know what you're talking about." Greyson looked at Brandon in fury and my heart stilled.

"It's time, Greyson. It's time we let everyone know the truth about the club." Brandon sighed and looked at me with bleak eyes. "And maybe then we can really try and seek some forgiveness."

AUTHOR'S NOTE

Thank you for reading *The Private Club* series. If you enjoyed the series, please leave a review.

There will be a follow-up series called *The Love Trials* starting in April 2014 that will focus on Nancy and the other secrets at *The Private Club*.

There is also a sequel coming out called *After The Ex Games* that provides insight into Brandon, Katie, Greyson, and Meg's lives. *After The Ex Games* and *The Private Club* Serials.

Please join my mailing list to be notified as soon as new books are released and to receive teasers: http://jscooperauthor.com/mail-list. You can find links and information about all my books here: http://jscooperauthor.com/books. I also love to interact with

readers on my Facebook page:
https://www.facebook.com/J.S.Cooperauthor.

As always, I love to here from new and old fans, please feel free to email me at any time at jscooperauthor@gmail.com.

ABOUT THE AUTHOR

J. S. Cooper was born in London, England and moved to Florida her last year of high school. After completing law school at the University of Iowa (from the sunshine to cold) she moved to Los Angeles to work for a Literacy non profit as an Americorp Vista. She then moved to New York to study the History of Education at Columbia University and took a job at a workers rights non profit upon graduation.

She enjoys long walks on the beach (or short), hot musicians, dogs, reading (duh) and lots of drama filled TV Shows.

Made in the USA
San Bernardino, CA
19 October 2014